One Year in Beijing

written by **Xiaohong Wang**

illustrated by **Grace Lin**

CHINA SPROUT
Chinese Cultural & Educational Products

My name is Ling Ling.
I am eight years old.

玲玲

my name in Chinese

CHINA

Beijing

I live in Beijing, the capital city of China. China is one of the largest countries in the world. Over 1.3 billion people live here. More people live in China than in any other country!

There are *three people* in my family: my mother, my father, and me. My dad works at a computer company and my mom is a teacher. We live in a modern high-rise apartment building. Most people in Beijing live in buildings like ours. There is a big, beautiful park nearby.

I love my neighborhood!

my apartment building

JANUARY

It's January 1st. Mom asks me to study hard for my exams in Chinese and math. I will take them later this month. Studying is very important to Chinese families! After our exams are over, we will start our winter break from school and get ready for Chinese New Year.

It's snowing outside. Mom takes me to Beihai Park to see the snow. Look at the beautiful white pagoda and the snow-covered mountain in the distance. Below, children ice skate on the frozen lake. See that big girl in the red outfit figure skating? I want to learn to skate like her!

Chinese New Year decorations

FEBRUARY - Chinese New Year has arrived!

This is a very important celebration for Chinese families. We clean our homes and make special preparations for the holiday. For Chinese New Year, families display spring couplets on our front door. Spring couplets are poems written in black or gold calligraphy on red paper. They express wishes for good fortune in the New Year.

On New Year's Eve, we make dumplings called jiaozi. Sometimes a coin is hidden in one of the jiaozi. Whoever finds it will have good luck in the New Year. Dumplings are my favorite food! This year, Mom teaches me how to make them.

On the morning of Chinese New Year, Mom gives me a small red envelope called hong bao. Maybe you've seen one! It contains a gift of money from my parents and grandparents that I can use to buy anything I want. This year I'll buy myself a Barbie doll. Chinese girls love Barbie dolls!

sweeping the house is an important tradition for the New Year

jiao zi

this is the doll I will buy myself

spring couplets

Another tradition to celebrate the New Year is the Lion Dance

my pinwheel

During the New Year, we go to the Di Tan Temple
Fair, where we buy beautiful crafts and traditional
Beijing snacks. I love tang hulu the most. Tang hulu is
skewered candied haws on a stick. As we are leaving,
Mom buys me a big paper pinwheel. I love Chinese
New Year!

tang hulu

On the streets, we see paper squares with the Chinese character Fu (Good Luck). They are hanging upside down. Mom says that the words "upside down good luck" have the same sound as the words "good luck arrival." It means that good luck is already here.

The 15th day of the New Year is the Lantern Festival. Today, my dad brings home sweet dumplings, called Yuanxiao. They are round and white. He says that they represent families being together. In the evening, we go to see a beautiful lantern show in the park. A lantern in the shape of a rabbit catches my eye. I was born in the Year of the Rabbit, so Mom buys it for me.

Yuanxiao

MARCH

The New Year's break is over and I'm back in school. I'm so excited to see my friends! Our teacher, Ms. Wang, asks us to write about something we enjoy. I write about our spring outing. When we are done, she hangs our compositions around the classroom. She is teaching us many new Chinese characters. Now that I've learned so many characters, I can write in my diary every day.

Red neckerchiefs used to be given to students for good behavior, but now everyone gets one.

Here are the Compositions We Wrote:

春节庙会   Chinese New Year Temple Fair

猜灯谜   Lantern Riddles

寒假的一天   One Day of Winter Break

美丽的春天   Beautiful Spring

春游   Spring Outing

我爱滑冰   I Love Ice Skating

我的同学   My Classmates

我最喜欢的书   My Favorite Book

APRIL

On Qing Ming Festival, Dad takes us to his hometown to visit our ancestors' tombs. This is a time when families remember loved ones who have passed away. He kowtows (bows) three times at his grandmother's tomb and then places fruit and cakes on it. He also burns some paper money. It's raining on the day of the festival. Mom says it often rains during Qing Ming because the heaven spirit, Lao Tian Ye, cries with all of us on this day.

Spring soon arrives. Our teacher asks us to observe the changes in nature around us. Pretty peach flowers are beginning to blossom. Young trees are starting to show tiny green buds. Kites are everywhere! Butterflies, goldfish, and dragons are flying in the sky. One man strings together many paper swallows to create a long and beautiful kite!

I wish I could fly a kite like that one!

peach blossom

this butterfly kite symbolizes love

MAY

May 1st is Labor Day. It is an important holiday in China because it honors working people all over the country! We have a week-long vacation from school. Mom and Dad take me to Shanxi by train. We visit some of the traditional houses

traditional houses

there. We also eat the famous Shanxi La Mian noodle that we buy from a food stand on the street. It's fun to watch the noodle man as he stretches and pulls the dough to create long, thin noodles. Then, he drops the noodle into a big pot of boiling water. When it's boiled, the noodle man mixes it with a delicious meat sauce.

When we return to school, the teacher tells us about a singing contest. It takes place every year and our school always participates. We sing traditional Chinese songs. We prepare by practicing for half an hour every day after school. On the day of the contest, we sing well and win second prize. I wish my mom and dad could come to hear us! But, they are working. They would be very proud of me.

JUNE

June 1st is International Children's Day. This holiday was started to celebrate children all over the world. In honor of Children's Day, Mom buys me a new shirt and a storybook about Snow White. Then, she takes me to the Children's Palace. We watch children singing and dancing and we play games. I play ring toss and get five rings on the peg! I win a stuffed panda. I wish every day was Children's Day!

my new shirt

On Duan Wu Jie (Dragon Boat Festival), I watch the boat races in the park. It is so exciting to watch the dragon boat teams compete! My favorite boat wins! On this day, Mom makes yummy Zong zi. Zong zi are sticky rice

dumplings wrapped in bamboo leaves and filled with red beans. Mom says we eat Zong zi to remember Qu Yuan, a hero poet from 2,000 years ago.

Zong zi

Qu Yuan

JULY

pedicab ride

at the Forbidden City

my cousin Wei Wei

Finally, school is over and summer vacation has arrived. My aunt's family, from Shanghai, comes to Beijing for a visit. My cousin, Wei Wei, is ten years old. We take them sightseeing. First, we hop into a pedicab and take a scenic ride around Shi Sha Hai Lake. Afterwards, we drink tea in one of Beijing's traditional courtyard.

Later, we visit the Great Wall, the Summer Palace, Tiananmen Square, and the Forbidden City.

Chinese tea set

Tiananmen Square

the Great Wall

the Summer Palace

These places were all built hundreds of years ago. They are a very important part of Chinese history, and we learn about them in school. I am glad that I can show them to Wei Wei.

AUGUST

The last week of summer break, my family takes a vacation to Yellow Mountain. We travel there by train. Dad says Yellow Mountain is one of the most beautiful places in the world!

We spend the whole day climbing the mountain but
only get halfway up by the end of the day, so we spend
the night in a big temple. The next day, we reach the
top. Dad is right. Yellow Mountain is spectacular!

SEPTEMBER

The Moon Festival is here. It falls on August 15th of the Chinese calendar. One of the traditions of the Moon Festival is for families to get together.

mooncake

We spend the holiday at my grandparent's courtyard house in Beijing. The festival always falls during the full moon, so we eat moon cakes by the light of the big, round moon.

Then, Mom tells me the story of the Moon Lady. At night, I dream that a little white bunny comes to my room and plays with me.

the Moon Lady

OCTOBER

China's National Day is October 1st. The People's Republic of China was founded on this day in 1949. Every year, we celebrate the birth of our country. On this day, Tiananmen Square is filled with huge flower arrangements that cover the square. Everyone loves to take pictures in front of the beautiful flowers.

maple leaf

During the National Day holiday, Mom, Dad, and I go to Fragrant Hills Mountain to see maple leaves. Mom shows us how to make bookmarks out of the leaves. I will send one to my cousin Wei Wei in Shanghai.

NOVEMBER

Fall passes quickly. November 5th is my birthday. Now I'm nine years old! I celebrate with my parents. Mom makes me a dish of "longevity noodles," which I eat at every birthday. Longevity noodles are very long noodles that you try to eat without breaking. Long noodles symbolize long life. Mom and Dad buy me a big birthday cake with "Happy Birthday" written on it. They also give me a birthday gift. Guess what they gave me? A pair of white ice skates! I can't wait until the weather turns cold so I can learn to skate.

skates

At school, our teacher is showing us how to use computers to log on to the Internet. I will try to send an email to Wei Wei in Shanghai. She has a computer, too.

DECEMBER

Winter has finally arrived! Snowflakes are flying everywhere. Our neighbors, Mei Mei and Ying Ying, are outdoors building a snowman and throwing snowballs. We have more and more homework now because final exams are coming.

It's December and we can see Christmas decorations in Beijing. Mom says many Westerners celebrate this holiday. But now Christmas has come to China! Many department stores even display and sell Christmas trees. We go to a Christmas party in a big hotel. Santa Claus brings many presents to the children. With "Silent Night" playing, we eat Christmas dinner, and I wonder what the year is like for kids in other countries.

FOOD

Jiaozi are Chinese Dumplings. Since the shape of jiaozi is similar to ancient Chinese money, called ingots, the Chinese believe that it symbolize wealth. Usually, families gather together to make dumplings on New Year's Eve. Even young children get to participate in making and rolling out the dough or spooning in the yummy filling. Sometimes, a coin is hidden inside one of the dumplings. The person who finds the coin is said to have good fortune in the New Year. Dumplings can be boiled or fried and the fillings can include anything from vegetables, to meat or seafood.

La Mian Noodle is a dish that originated in the Shanxi Province. Shanxi is famous for its many varieties of noodles. La Mian is a kind of noodle that is pulled by hand. The noodle is soft, smooth, and chewy. It can be pulled into different thicknesses. After cooking, it is served with a variety of meat or vegetable sauces.

Longevity Noodles symbolize long life and are often served on birthdays, Chinese New Year, and other important holidays. Be careful not to break them! The longer the better!

Mooncakes are served for the Moon Festival, which is also called Mid-Autumn Festival. Often, mooncakes are stamped with Chinese characters and are made of a flaky pastry shell. They are frequently filled with red bean paste, lotus paste, nuts, and hams. Sometimes, dried, salted egg yolks or other tasty fillings are also baked inside.

Tang Hu Lu means "sugary gourd". This traditional Chinese treat is made by skewering candied hawthorn berries (haws) on a stick. Haws are the size of a very large marble. During Chinese New Year, many vendors line the street selling this traditional, ancient candy.

Yuanxiao, also called sweet dumpling, is served during the Lantern Festival. It is made with sticky rice and filled with sweet stuffing. Yuanxiao is round in shape, symbolizing family unity, wholeness and happiness. The Lantern Festival (Yuanxiao Jie) is named after this delicious dumpling.

Zong Zi is a sticky rice dumpling wrapped in bamboo or reed leaves. This traditional Chinese food is made for Duan Wu Jie (Dragon Boat Festival). Savory meat and vegetables, sweet dates, or bean paste fill the center of the sticky rice. The fillings for Zong Zi vary from region to region.

HOLIDAYS

Chinese New Year is the most celebrated holiday in China. Also known as the Spring Festival, it is a time when families get together to celebrate the arrival of a new year. Before the New Year, families clean their homes and purchase new clothing to start the year fresh. They also hang couplets on their walls and doors. Friends and families enjoy daily New Year's feasts throughout the two-week holiday. In Beijing, there are many temple fairs where people go to celebrate, purchase beautiful crafts, enjoy wonderful entertainers, and eat delicious food.

Dragon Boat Festival began almost 2,000 years ago to honor a man named Qu Yuan. He was a wise poet and politician who drowned himself to protest government corruption. When people heard that he had thrown himself in the water, they raced out in their long boats hoping to find him. This tradition continues today on the anniversary of Qu Yuan's death. People celebrate the festival by racing dragon boats and eating Zong Zi. Dragon boats are long, narrow boats. They are brightly colored, and have a dragon-shaped head and a long tail.

International Children's Day is celebrated on June 1st. Children's Day was started in 1949 to draw attention to issues involving children and to bring them joy and a sense of national pride. It is a day of great fun for children in China. Schools put on pageants and throw parties. Many theaters, museums, and parks are open for free to children.

Labor Day is an annual holiday celebrating working people. It occurs on May 1st. Workers all across China are given three days off to rest. Many people use this time to travel, shop, or enjoy themselves.

Moon Festival, also called Mid-Autumn Festival, is a day that families gather together. This is the second most important festival in China. Moon Festival always falls on August 15th on the Chinese lunar calendar. The moon is especially bright on this evening and people sit gazing at it and eating sweet mooncakes. Children play with festive lanterns and sometimes get to stay up until midnight when the Chinese believe that the moon is at its roundest.

National Day is the anniversary of the founding of the People's Republic of China in 1949. All across China, people hold parades to celebrate. City streets and squares are decorated with Chinese national flags and flowers. At night, there are beautiful fireworks. Many people get a few days off of work and school in honor of this important occasion that unified the country.

Qing Ming Festival, also called the Clear and Bright Festival, is a time to show respect for the deceased. During this festival, many people travel to visit the graves of their ancestors. They clean off the gravesites and take a walk in the countryside. Special offerings, such as bowls of fruit, cakes and fresh flowers are placed on the grave and fake money, called joss paper, is burned.

PLACES

Beihai Park is one of the most popular parks in Beijing. For almost 800 years, this park served as the royal garden of the Jin, Yuan, Ming, and Qing Dynasties. Beihai Park is home to many historic structures including the Jade Bowl Pavilion, the Nine Dragon Screen, and the Five Dragon Pavilion. During the winter, people come to skate and take in the beautiful, snowy scenery.

Di Tan Temple Fair takes place around the Chinese New Year. It is one of Beijing's four main fairs. Di Tan is also known as Temple of the Earth. Over one million people visit Di Tan during the celebration, so it is a popular place for merchants to sell their wares. Visitors to the fair can purchase handicrafts like kites, papercuts, paintings, and children's toys. They can also enjoy local snacks and live entertainment such as acrobats and magicians.

The Forbidden City is also called the Palace Museum. It is located in the exact center of Beijing. The Forbidden City was built almost 600 years ago. It was the imperial palace during the Ming and Qing Dynasties and was the home to many emperors. The Forbidden City was opened to the public in 1950. It is one of the most popular tourist spots in the world.

Fragrant Hills Mountain is located just outside of Beijing. It was first built almost 800 years ago and covers almost 400 acres. The park features cable cars, pagodas, stone bridges, and walking trails that wind through beautiful natural scenery. In the autumn, as the leaves change color, the mountains are covered with fiery red, yellow, and orange trees.

The Great Wall is one of the most famous architectural artifacts in the world. It was built to protect the people of China from invading Mongol nomads. The earliest part of the wall was built over 2,000 years ago. At one time, the Wall extended almost 5,000 miles across China. Today, only 1,500 miles of the Wall remains. The most visited portion of the Great Wall is outside of Beijing. It attracts tens of thousand of visitors every day.

Hutongs are narrow alleys that run between the traditional homes of Beijing residents. The homes along the hutongs were first built over 700 years ago. Each home consists of a rectangular courtyard that is surrounded on each side by a one story, tile roof building. Today, many courtyard homes are being replaced by large apartment buildings to accommodate the many people of Beijing.

The Summer Palace is one of the most noted classical gardens in the world. The garden was originally built almost 900 years ago. Over the centuries, many imperial families added to it and used the garden as a luxurious resort for rest and entertainment. Empress Dowager Cixi rebuilt the garden after a terrible fire and changed its name to Summer Palace (Yiheyuan). She lived there during her later years handling government affairs and entertaining.

Tiananmen Square is one of the largest public squares in the world. It can hold up to a million people and has been host to some of China's most important ceremonies. Tiananmen Square is named for its majestic "Gate of Heavenly Peace" and serves as one of the entrances to the Forbidden City.

Yellow Mountain (Huangshan) is located in the southern part of the Anhui Province, in eastern China. It is famous for its breathtaking scenery and is one of the most popular tourist spots in the country. Elegant pine and cypress trees cover the many mountain peaks. The three tallest peaks, Lotus Flower Peak, Ever Bright Peak, and Heavenly Capital Peak, are often shrouded in a low-hanging sea of clouds. This makes them a favorite subject of artists.

TRADITIONS

The Moon Lady is known as Chang'e in Chinese. She is considered to be the goddess of the moon. Chang'e was married to an archer named Hou Yi. One day, 10 suns arose in the sky, burning the earth and causing droughts and famines. The emperor called upon Hou Yi to help and he shot nine of the suns out of the sky. In return for his bravery, the emperor gave Hou Yi a pill, to share with his wife, which would allow them to live forever. Hou Yi went home and hid the pill but before he could take it, Chang'e's curiosity overcame her and she swallowed the pill herself. Quickly, she began floating and ascended to the moon, where she lives on forever. A jade rabbit keeps her company, continually working to create an elixir of life.

The Chinese Zodiac represents a 12-year cycle of time. Each of the 12 years in the Chinese zodiac is named after a different animal. The zodiac animal signs are the rat, ox, tiger, rabbit, dragon, snake, horse, sheep (or goat), monkey, rooster, dog, and pig. Many Chinese believe that the year of a person's birth determines their personality traits and the amount of success and happiness the person will have in life.

Written in Chinese by Xiaohong Wang
Translated by Lei Li
Edited by Myra Alperson & Bethann Buddenbaum

Text copyright © 2006 by ChinaSprout, Inc.
Illustrations copyright © 2006 by Grace Lin
Book Designed by Grace Lin

Publisher's Cataloging-in-Publication
Wang, Xiaohong, 1966-
One year in Beijing / written by Xiaohong Wang; illustrated by Grace Lin.
p. cm.
SUMMARY: A year-long journey in the world of Ling Ling,
a young girl who lives in Beijing, China. Her
personal accounts tell about Chinese culture, including
school life, family life, and holidays and festivals.
Audience: Ages 4-8.
ISBN 0-9747302-5-4
1. China--Social life and customs--Juvenile fiction.
2. Children--China--Juvenile fiction.
[1. China--Fiction. 2. Beijing (China)--Fiction. 3. Manners andcustoms--Fiction.
4. Children--China--Fiction. 5. Family--China--Fiction.]
I. Lin, Grace. II. Title.
PZ7.W1812One 2006 [E] QBI06-600175

Printed in Singapore
First Edition, 2006
10 9 8 7 6 5 4 3 2 1
ChinaSprout, Inc.
www.chinasprout.com